Fι

In memory of
Professor Steven Collins,
a true *paṇḍita*

Also by Nigel Tetley

Contents

Acknowledgements

'The Actor's Soliloquy', 'A Bubble of Perfection' and 'The Perfect Crime' first made their appearance in *When Bees Flew in for Breakfast* (The Choir Press, 2016), but I have taken this opportunity of a second collection to make slight improvements to them.

Modified versions of, 'The Thief' and 'Summon the Scholars!' were first published by Encore Publications as texts of two Christmas carols under the titles, 'Snow' and 'The Way of Paradox' respectively (music by Neil Porter-Thaw). Both texts are here reprinted by kind permission of the publisher (copyright, Encore Publications, 2006).

Zero

Have you ever wondered why a nought looks like a hole,
An empty, gaping, open mouth dug neatly by a mole?

Now every hole that's ever found is always just the same:
A round and airy space where nothing's found that you can
name.

Just like the holes in yellow cheese, or doughnuts that you eat,
Or tea-cup handles, round and slim, or worn out socks on feet.

So could it be that zero has the look of what it means?
That it shows a hollow space like an empty can of beans?

For when all numbers disappear and leave a vacant space,
What's left is simply nothing, nought, like zero's blank, white
face!

A Sense of Direction

In the process of seed germination,
There is knowledge of orientation,
For up go all shoots,
And down go all roots,
Like an in-built, bipolar relation.

But no seed has a head or a toe,
So how could they possibly know,
Sitting deep underground,
With a shape small and round,
Where up is as opposed to below?

Now You See It, Now You Don't

It floated in the harbour where Piraeus met the sea,
The ship once sailed by heroes, it is said,
The splendid Ship of Theseus was moored beside the quay,
Its beauty turned each passing person's head.

But unbeknown to all who daily gazed upon the ship,
A plot was being hatched each dead of night,
By moonlight, men would climb aboard to steal it, snip by snip,
Replacing what they'd filched with skilful sleight.

Plank by plank and sail by sail, each part was nightly taken,
But no-one smelled a whiff of dark, foul play,
By day, the ship looked just the same, it could not be mistaken,
The small change made no difference either way.

The thieves continued night by night, not leaving any trails,
They carried on until their work was done,
They'd stolen every shipshape part – the mastheads, planks and
    sails,
By taking and replacing every one.

The stolen parts were stockpiled high awaiting reconstruction,
At which the men all laboured as one crew,
They re-assembled all the parts like copycat abduction,
Until the ship once more stood proud and true.

And then one day the men enacted this, their final act,
They moored it in the harbour so to take,
Now *two* ships floated side by side in every way exact,
And each one seemed to be both real and fake.

"That neither is the former ship is plain for all to see,"
The men declared as one united team,
"The famous Ship of Theseus has gone and ceased to be,
So *both* are ours and *both* we now redeem!"

A Question of Probity

Could it be that all money is counterfeit?
It's hard to disprove if you think a bit,
No bank is endorsed by a Holy Writ,
So *why* do we trust every bit of it?

Could it be every banker's a hypocrite?
Minting valueless cash for the sake of it?
Making all of us think quite the opposite?
When toiling to stave off a credit hit?

It's a mind-blowing thought to consider it,
That currencies worldwide are counterfeit,
To call it a scam might be apposite,
So why don't we all just get rid of it?

The Registrar

I am making a list of all things unlisted,
A record of all things left out,
My archive will be of such perfect completion,
That nothing will then be in doubt.

My work may be noble, but progress is hard,
Each time that I act, I'm resisted,
For as soon as a newly found item is entered,
It loses its status, 'unlisted'.

Each entry I make I then have to delete,
My list is a blank page negation,
A catalogue made up of what it is not,
Like hunger appeased by starvation.

All items deleted are once more unlisted,
And forever located elsewhere,
The realm of excluded is strangely elusive,
Like mapping the contours of air.

So far, I've identified forty such things,
(An oddly assorted farrago,)
But setting them down simply cannot be done,
For such is their audit embargo.

I am caught in a difficult logical loop,
With experts I need to consult,
But at least all my labours thus far are transparent,
Overleaf, I reveal the result.

A List of All Things Unlisted

1. –
2. –
3. –
4. –
5. –
6. –
7. –
8. –
9. –
10. –
11. –
12. –
13. –
14. –
15. –
16. –
17. –
18. –
19. –
20. –
21. –
22. –
23. –
24. –
25. –
26. –
27. –
28. –
29. –
30. –
31. –
32. –

33. –
34. –
35. –
36. –
37. –
38. –
39. –
40. –

The Actor's Soliloquy

I am not who I am,
And I am who I'm not,
I'm a living and stark contradiction,
I express what is true,
Yet my life is a lie,
I'm a fact even though I'm a fiction,
Every move that I make
Is an act of pretence,
A sham from beginning to end,
A sheer fabrication,
A glorified lie,
Whenever I play *Let's Pretend*,
There is no human drama
I cannot take part in,
I perform every role unrestricted,
But alone in my room,
There's no sign of myself,
Like a tenant now long since evicted,
My essence is merely
Dramatis Personae,
A bundle of roles with no core,
An identity void
Of a real, solid self,
A collection of parts, nothing more,
So when I use the word 'I'
In the course of a script,
What is meant by this pronoun's grammatical span?
Am I me when I act or somebody else?
Just who is now speaking:
The mask or the man?

The Sun

Have
you
ever
wondered
why
the
sun
that
shines
up
in
the
sky
seems
to
look
so
very
small
and
never
very
big
at
all?

It
has
always
seemed
to
me
a
real
and
total
mystery
of
how
the
sun
that
shines
up
high
can
warm
the
earth,
the
sea
and
sky.

How
can
the
sun
that
shines
up
high
be
quite
so
bright
and
hot
when
all
it
ever
looks
like
is
a
small
and
yellow
dot?

Why
isn't
the
sun
as
big
as
a
house?
Why
is
it
the
size
of
a
mole
or
a
mouse?

The
sun
is
so
strong
that
it
kills
off
the
night,
yet
it's
only
the
size
of
a
bee
in
mid
flight.

The size of the sun
Should be huge and gigantic,
Like a hot air balloon,
Or the Ocean Atlantic.

But
it
seems
that
the
sun's
not
as
big
as
the
sea,
for
it's
only
the
size
of
a
single,
round
pea.

But
why
it
should
be
that
the
sun
is

as
wee
as
a
flea
or
a
chimpanzee's
left
or
right
knee
(or
even
an
apple
that
hangs
from
a
tree)
is
a
totally
puzzling,
utterly
baffling,
deep
and
inscrutable
mystery
to
me.

Uninvited Guest

What does it want with me?
What are its motives?
Why won't it leave me alone?
I do not know how to interpret its presence,
Is it playful or violently prone?

It raps on the windows
And pounds the front door
Like a frantic and unwelcome guest,
But I daren't let it in, I ignore its persistence,
But, strangely, I am at its behest.

With no will of my own,
I sit at my window
Still fearful of any intrusion,
But soon I am lured by its masterclass play
Of art forms in endless profusion.

Surrealist fusions
Of textures and forms
Trickle down from the frame to the ledge,
As droplets re-work the grey canvas
By dissolving each linear edge.

Pinbursts of
Concentric geometry
Dance and glide on all puddles in sight,
Transforming each celluloid surface
Into vanishing ringlets of light.

From the safety
Of an old, black umbrella,
I venture outside to see more,
But I'm shocked by the improvised rhythms
Of percussion without any score.

From the metronome
Thud of the rhubarb,
To the pavestones' sharp, dissonant spluttering,
Each flowerbed's legato-light patter
Times the overflow crash of the guttering.

And through it all
I can sense up above me,
A libretto being typed out at speed,
As the effervescent fizz on my umbrella
Taps the carbonated print of the screed.

My guest seems
Benign after all,
And, what's more, a real genius at play,
But what, I repeat, are its motives,
When all its efforts are clean washed away?

Once

The gaze once so bewitching
    no longer casts a spell,
The face once rich in narrative
    has nothing left to tell.

The walk that once defined the space
    no longer seems to dance,
The touch once charged with heady risk
    no longer stands a chance.

The voice once so pitch-perfect
    no longer makes a sound,
The poise once gently buoyant
    lies beached and run aground.

The smiles that once besieged the heart
    no longer catch the eye,
The presence once mysterious
    has lost the question why.

The entrance that once swayed the room
    no longer turns the head,
Her countenance has turned to dust,
    his love for her is dead.

Up and Down

What *can't* go down a chimney up,
But *can* go up it down?
If you can solve this riddle,
You've the smartest brain in town!

My Reflection

When I look into a mirror,
I can always clearly see
A person staring back
Who looks exactly just like me.

He's called, 'My Own Reflection,'
And he lives in every mirror,
He also lives in ponds and lakes
And sometimes in a river.

My reflection always looks like me,
Morning, noon and night,
Except for just one tiny thing:
My left is on his right.

My reflection is the same as me,
Except he's in reverse,
Our lefts and rights are crossways round,
It's almost like a curse.

He copies every move I make,
My walk, my smile, my nodding head,
But when I raise my right hand high,
Up goes his left instead.

Oh, why do mirrors play this trick
Of swapping left and right,
When they never flip round up and down,
Or even black and white?

My question is much harder so
Than drawing oblong squares,
Or even walking on your hands
To climb a flight of stairs.

But what if mirrors *did* flip round
Both up and down and black and white,
Or even played the crafty trick
Of switching day for night?

We'd never know what time it was,
Or when to sleep or play,
We wouldn't even have a clue
Of where the firm ground lay.

So I'm glad that my reflection's
Only flipped around one way,
Or I might think that I'm upside-down,
Or worse: that night is day.

The Thief

It came in the stealth of the night,
In the silence of a perfect conspiracy,
With the touch of a thief it stole softly,
Leaving nothing behind but a mystery.

It stilled and becalmed all before it,
Before furtively hiding its treasure,
In the shroud of a white, untold secret,
Beyond all comprehension or measure.

We woke to a blinding concealment,
And a deafening absence of sound,
Nothing was left but the debris
Of the plunder that lay all around.

The staccato sharp crunch of my footsteps
Then imprinted their way out of sight,
And remained as the final deception,
As the trail of the thief of the night.

A Question of Taste

I cannot abide coriander,
To me, it's but herb propaganda,
When it touches my tongue,
It's like soap mixed with dung,
Neither sauce for the goose nor the gander!

But all chefs who cook here on this Earth,
Seem to think it's the next Virgin Birth,
From Moroccan tagines,
To Mexican beans,
People worship its culinary worth.

I am told that I have a rogue gene,
That makes coriander obscene,
What foul, fake news sneakery,
To cast me as freakery,
The fault's in the plant, not my protein!

And the Difference Is?

Pulse,
Pitch,
Dynamics,
Tonality,
Tempo,
Phrasing,
Timbre and Timing,
Register,
Rhythm,
Rubato and Breathing,
Always linguistic but not always rhyming.

Modulation,
Inflection,
Projection and Placement,
Melody,
Story and Accented Diction,
Rests,
Repeats,
Resonance,
Dissonance,
A narrative line,
Fact and/or Fiction.

These are the elements of what we call *singing*,
A full definition with nothing left out,
This is a list exhaustive and true:
The meaning of *singing* without any doubt.

Pulse,
Pitch,
Dynamics,
Tonality,
Tempo,
Phrasing,
Timbre and Timing,
Register,
Rhythm,
Rubato and Breathing,
Always linguistic but not always rhyming.

Modulation,
Inflection,
Projection and Placement,
Melody,
Story and Accented Diction,
Rests,
Repeats,
Resonance,
Dissonance,
A narrative line,
Fact and/or Fiction.

These are the elements of what we call *speaking*,
A full definition with nothing left out,
This is a list exhaustive and true:
The meaning of *speaking* without any doubt.

The Chasm

Imagine a chasm
With no physical limit,
Of no known geological form,
No structure or strata,
No climate or movement,
The inverted stone eye of a storm.

Imagine a chasm
That cannot be bridged,
Of infinite, vertical drop,
An unyielding gulf
That goes on for ever,
No bottom, no sides and no top.

Imagine a chasm
With no colour or light,
Where all trace of life is destroyed,
An emptiness, empty
Of even itself,
A cold, static, monochrome void.

Now imagine this chasm
And concentrate hard
Until the image is fixed hard and set,
Then explore its dimensions
With all of your senses,
And you will know
How it feels
To regret.

A Bubble of Perfection

Nothing is as perfect as a bubble,
A faulty bubble simply cannot be,
You will never find a bubble
That is dented, scratched or broken,
Such an apparition you will never see.

Mathematically a bubble is unequalled,
Its surface is a geometric wonder,
It's as infinite in tangents
As identical in angles,
This is $4\pi r^2$ without a blunder.

Its curvature is absolute exactitude,
An equibalanced sphere of pure delight,
As elusive as a shadow,
And as fragile as a prayer,
Or an uncorrupted thought that's taken flight.

The beauty of a bubble can't be captured
When plotted on the axes: x, y, z,
Its co-ordinates are endless,
It defies full definition,
Like the meaning of a tune that can't be said.

A bubble can exist in air or liquid,
Drifting down or gently floating to the top,
But this happy ball of fun
Has a tragic, hidden nature,
For just as it gets going, it goes POP!

The Perfect Crime

Three Bedouin nomads made their way through hostile desert
As their sandy trail meandered out of sight,
They had travelled many miles and their camels now were
    weary,
So the three men stopped to pitch tents for the night.

They built a fire and cooked a meal and tethered all their camels,
Then one by one each man prepared for bed,
And to all outside appearances the men were best of friends,
But the truth was one would soon be killed stone dead.

The victim of this evil crime was one Mahmood Masood,
And on that fateful night at peace he slept
Unaware that his companions were intent upon his murder,
As one by one into his tent they crept.

The first man poured out poison into Mahmood's skin canteen
That contained his one supply of fresh spring water,
The man knew that Mahmood would surely need to quench his
    thirst,
Thus the desert heat would bring about his slaughter.

Happily convinced he'd put an end to Mahmood's life,
The man returned to bed without a sound,
Unaware that he was not alone in wanting Mahmood dead
As the second man crawled snake-like on the ground.

This second man crawled stealthily right into Mahmood's tent,
And in his mouth he held a sharpened knife,
He used the knife to pierce small holes in Mahmood's skin
    canteen,
Thus draining Mahmood's water and his life.

Then he crawled back to his tent like a silent, deadly viper,
Leaving Mahmood's canteen dripping in the sand,
A dreadful act of murder had been carried out this night,
But the question was by which deceptive hand?

Mahmood's poor, dead body was discovered three days later,
He had died of lack of water, it was said,
His two erstwhile companions were caught up with and
    arrested,
They were each asked why Mahmood should now be dead.

Each man then independently confessed his evil deed,
Which made all legal hearts begin to race,
For no-one could establish who the murderer could be,
Were intentions linked to outcomes in this case?

The greatest judge in all the land was called to try the case,
He was learnèd and his judgements were incisive,
He sifted all the evidence, yet only found confusion,
But nonetheless his verdict was decisive.

"As soon as Mahmood's water had been poisoned he was
    finished,"
The Judge observed when summing up the case,
"But the actions of the second man then undermined this plan,
It's as if the killer had no human face."

"Neither man is innocent, but neither man is guilty,"
The Judge continued wasting little time,
"The killer of Mahmood Masood will never be determined,
I declare his death to be the perfect crime."

Christmas Trilogy

I: *In a Time of Prophecy*

We'll take it, withstand it,
Hold fast and endure it,
Grit our teeth, tough it out,
Persevere and survive it,
We'll resist, we'll be strong,
We'll be wise and far-sighted,
We will exercise patience,
We'll be stoic and calm,
We will wait in the silence
Without thought of complaint,
We will wait in the fog
And the cold and the waste,
We will not make a sound,
We'll lie dormant and still,
We will witness our fear
So as not to give in,
We will wait, we will wait,
And we'll wait and we'll wait,
We won't move, we won't flinch,
We will pray through despair:
That the pain of a birth
Will tear open the night,
And the day breaks at last
To a breath of fresh air.

II: Summon the Scholars!

Summon the scholars!
Commission all views!
Re-write the textbooks!
Consult every Muse!

The laws of our governance
No longer hold sway,
The world has been altered
On this Christmas day.

The grammatical I
No longer exists,
Three is now One,
And no logic persists.

No compass direction
Gives orientation,
All solitary travel
Has lost its duration.

The Earth has changed orbit
Through one act of love,
All order's upturned,
What was low is above.

All age is suspended:
Each calendar date,
Time's Scythe and its Glass
Lie smashed at His Gate.

Tell all whom you see
In the town and the street
Of this New Dispensation,
Tell all whom you meet.

This new, upturned world
Is to me quite unknown,
But I know through unknowing
We're no longer alone.

Summon the scholars!
Commission all views!
Re-write the textbooks!
Consult every Muse!

The laws of our governance
No longer hold sway,
The world has been altered
On this Christmas day.

III: Epiphany

What were they thinking,
Those men from the East,
When they left their estates and their wives and their homes,
With their bags stuffed with star maps,
Predictions and numbers,
And dense, theoretical theses and tomes?

What were they thinking,
Those men from the East,
On their scholarly-led and declared expedition?
When they charted the planets
And decoded the night,
Did they sense they were nearing some new erudition?

What were they thinking,
Those men from the East,
When surveying the passing and varied terrain?
Did they misconstrue nothing?
Were they so self-assured
That all knowledge was theirs as a prize one could gain?

What were they thinking,
Those men from the East,
Taking stock of their rarefied talents and gifts?
Did they ponder their meaning?
Take delight in their worth?
Did such thoughts lead to arguments, contests and rifts?

What were they thinking,
Those men from the East,
When their caravan tired and pitched tents for the night?
Sipping sherbet in cities
As crowned, honoured guests,
Did they feel such attention was fitting and right?

So is that what they thought,
Those men from the East?
Then were they, like me, nearly broken with shame,
When alighting at last,
At the point of arrival,
They found that He knew them already, by name?